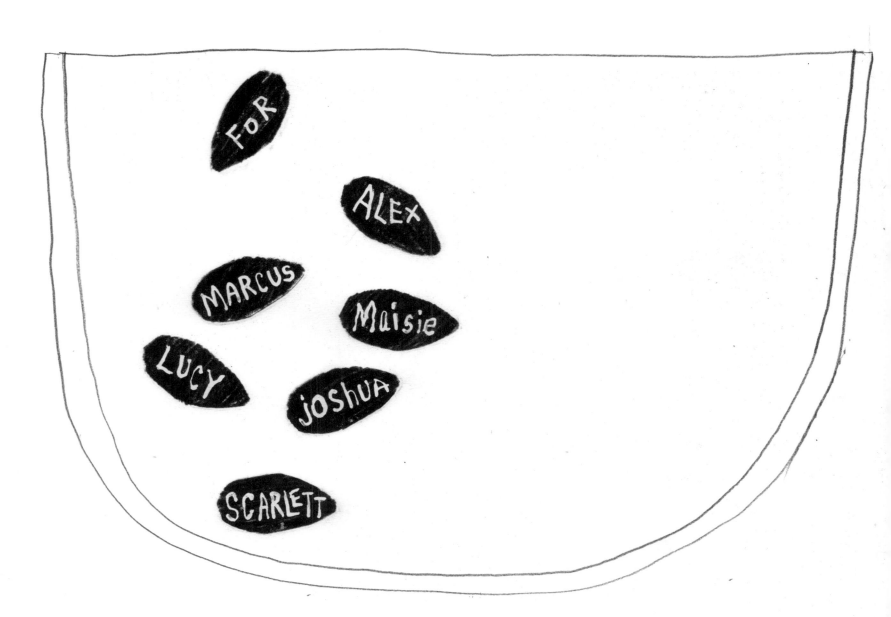

ALEX and the Watermelon Boat

Chris McKimmie

Allen & Unwin

But I had to go outside.

Rabbit, my most favourite stuffed toy, had hopped out the window and was gone.

I had to go after him.

Outside, the river had burst its banks.

The dam was OVERFLOWING. The water was rising.

300 SPRING ROLLS

FISH 70 FINGERS

200 TV DINNERS FOR 2

PIZZA 60 FROZEN 60

NO. 1000 BAKED BEANS

The rain had gone away but the clouds were **heavy** and **BIG.**

Binky the cat was **stuck on the roof with nothing to eat.**

Merilyn Kafoops and Dyson the dog were cooking up a storm on the BBQ.
But where was the other Kafoops twin?

And where was Rabbit?

All the shops were empty.

A robber was stealing sausages from Barry and no one was stopping him.

I couldn't stop him. I had to find Rabbit.

Scarlett was floating away in her afternoon bath and didn't care a bit. Molly the cow was lost. Where was Baby Wally? And where was Rabbit?

Rabbit was not on the freeway.
Nothing was moving there.
Everything was jammed up.
There was a shark in the way.

I had lost
Rabbit.

Lonely Ross had lost one boot.

And then
all the lights in
the world went
out.

I was lost.

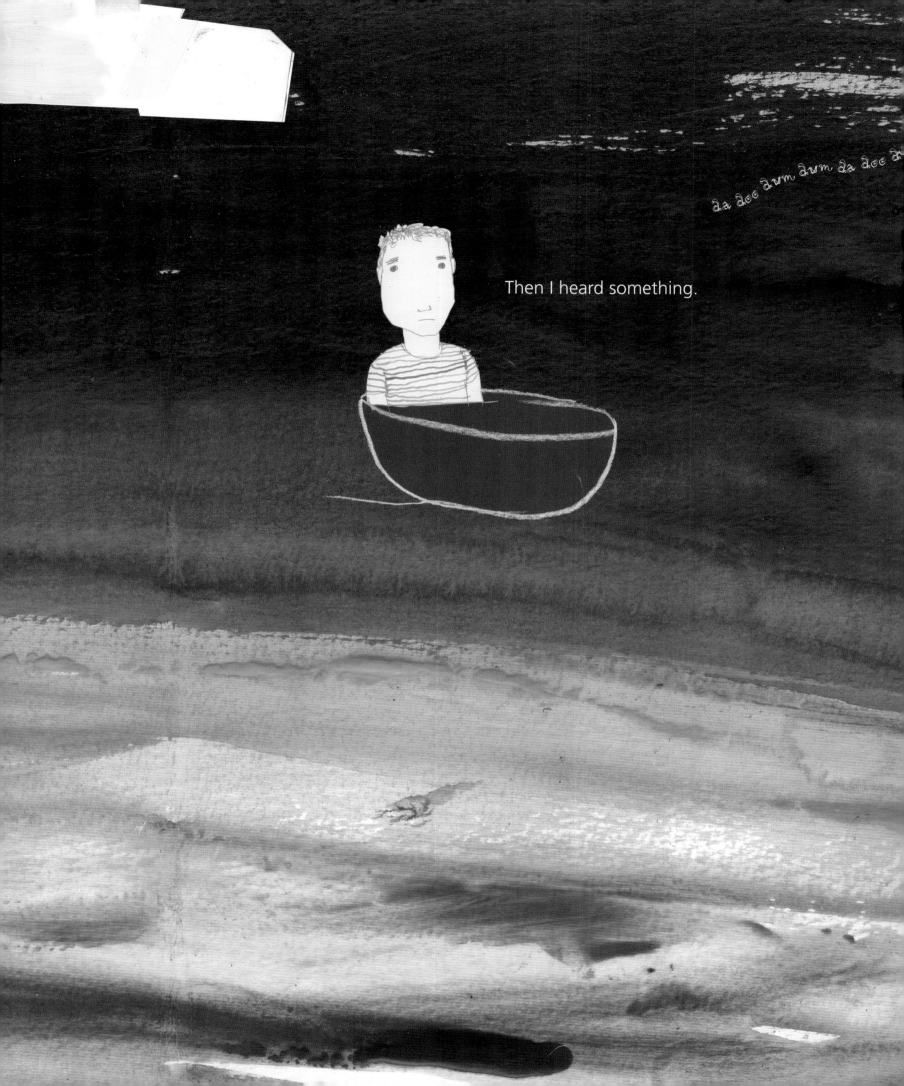

Then I heard something.

da doo dum dum da doo d

dum dum da doooo dummmm da doo dum dum da doo du
HELP!
I knew Rabbit was here somewhere.

And he was.

I
wanted
to
keep
on
going
but
Rabbit
was
too
tired.

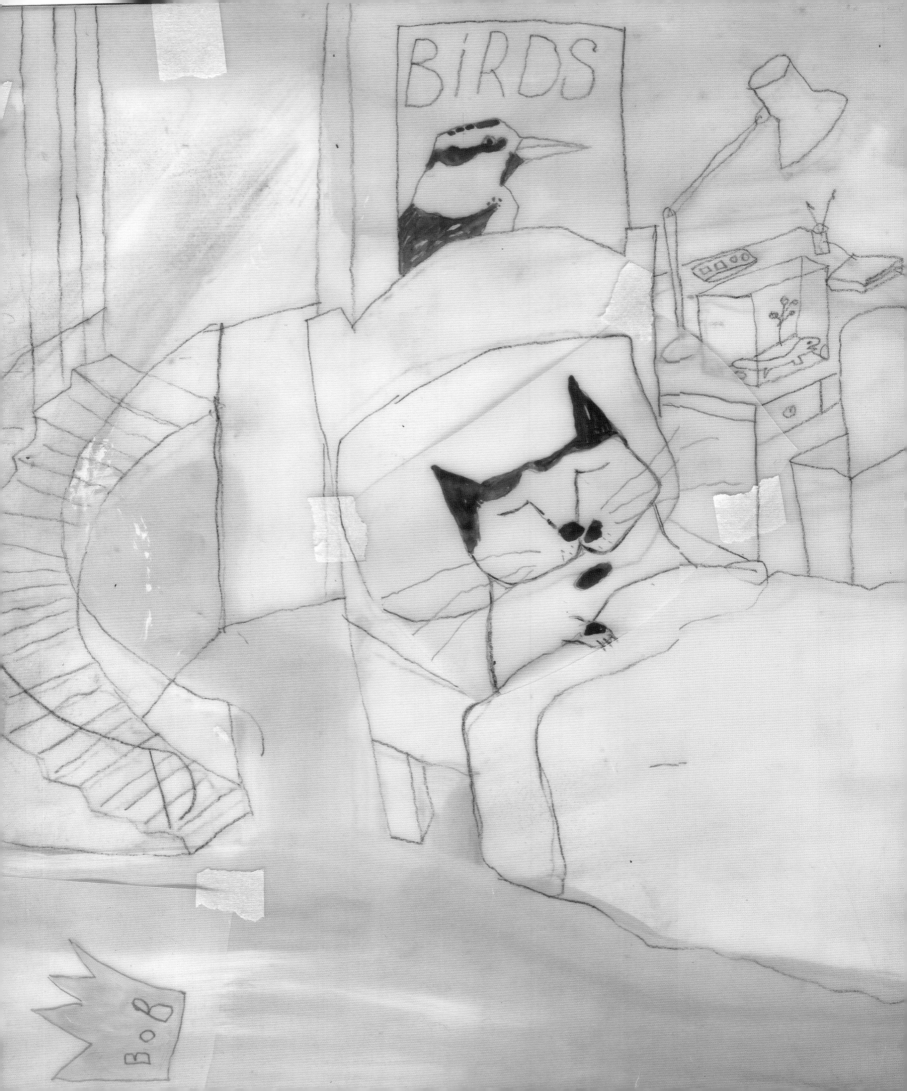

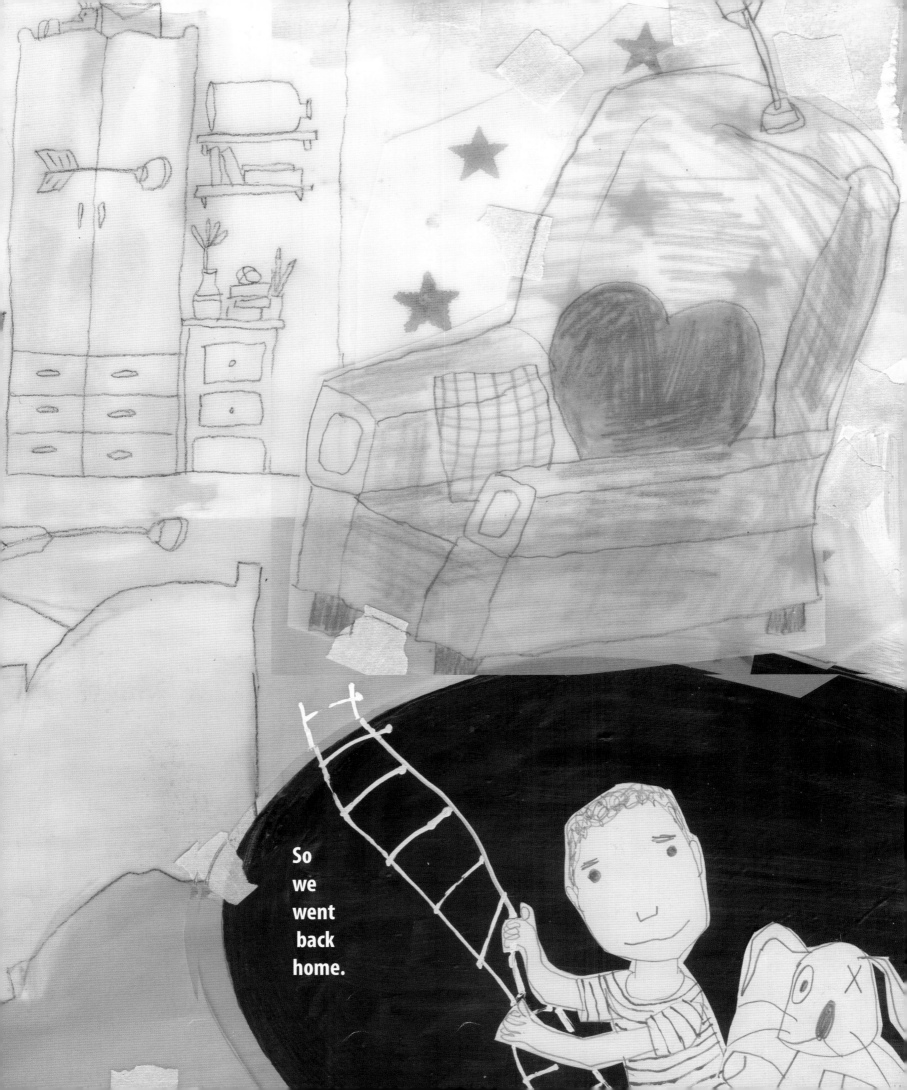

So
we
went
back
home.

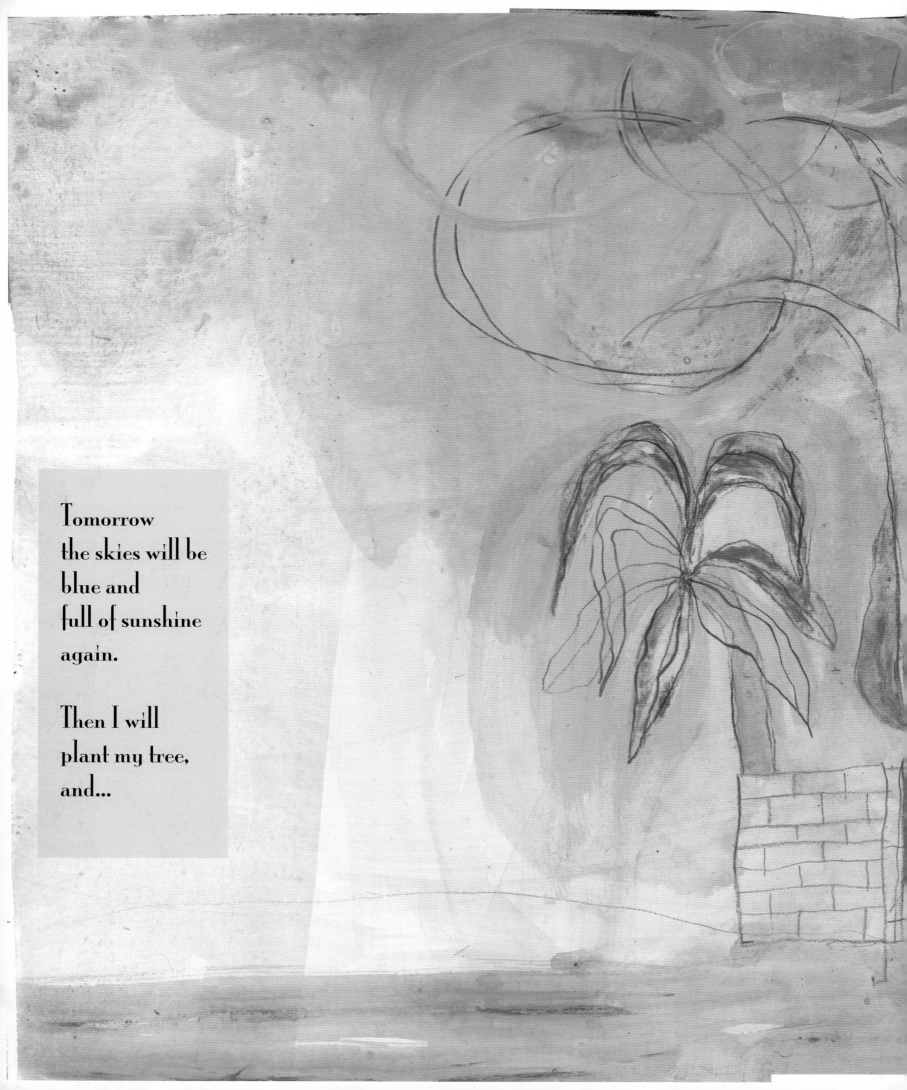

Tomorrow
the skies will be
blue and
full of sunshine
again.

Then I will
plant my tree,
and...

when it grows
big all
the birds
will come
back.

Acrylic paint
Water Colour
Gouache
House paint
Pastels
Oil pastels
Ink
Coloured Pencils
Pencils
Tracing Paper
MASKing TAPE
Sticky tape
mdf BOARD
Star stamp
biro and stencils.
WHITE OUT PEN

Alex McKimmie drew the bird
on the title page
and wrote and drew the tree
planting instructions on the
last endpaper.
Alex also did the lettering
for the words
'I was lost.'

Maisie McKimmie drew the little
figure in the watermelon
on the title page.
Maisie also made the little house
with the red door that is on
the bottom of the page
that has the shark on the freeway.

Thanks, once again, to
Susannah and Erica.

Maisie
made her
house out of
Balsa wood
and nails
and painted
it.

ISBN: 978 1 743310076

This book was printed in January 2012 at
Tien Wah Press (PTE) Limited,
TWP SDN BHD, TAMPOI
No. 89 Jalan Tampoi
Kawasan Perindustrian Tampoi
80350 Johor Bahru

10 9 8 7 6 5 4 3 2 1

A Cataloguing-in-Publication entry is
available from the National Library of Australia
www.trove.nia.gov.au

Allen & Unwin
83 Alexander Street Crows Nest
NSW 2065 Australia.
Phone: (61 2) 8425 0100
Fax: (61 2) 9906 2218
E mail: info@allenandunwin.com
Web: www.allenandunwin.com

Instructi

1. water the plants

2. Let the sun

3. The plant will
will be happy.